9/98

Wow* I Got to go to the North Pole

The Best Christmas Wish of All

As reported by
R. W. (Bob) Thompson, Jr.
illustrated by
Roderick K. Keitz
and published by
The North Pole Chronicles

"After all, things don't happen at the North Pole just at Christmastime."

It was **Christmas** Eve and I was sound asleep, dreaming of all of the things
I hoped Santa Claus would bring me.

When I wrote my letter telling him everything I wanted for Christmas, I told Santa
that I write a newspaper to pass out to my friends in the neighborhood.
I said I wanted some stories about things that had happened at the North Pole
so I could put them in my paper.
They didn't have to be about things that happened just at Christmas,
they could be about things that happened at any time of the year.

A good newspaper always tells stories about things
people want to know about.

Suddenly, I felt someone shake me and say, "Hurry, wake up."

When I opened my eyes, standing right there beside my bed
was Santa Claus himself.
Was it really him, or was I still dreaming?

"Come along with me and you can get all of the stories you want," Santa said.
"But you must hurry and get dressed
so I can finish delivering toys to all of the other girls and boys."
Wow! I sure wasn't still dreaming.

I don't always get everything I want for Christmas, but I never really thought
I would be lucky enough to get stories for my paper right from the North Pole.
"I must have been a very good boy this year," I thought.
"This time I asked for the impossible and got it!"

After leaving a letter telling my family where I was going and putting on my heaviest
coat, Santa and I climbed onto his sleigh and we were soon up, up, and away.
Before I could catch my breath or realize what was happening,
we were already landing at the North Pole.

Many of the elves were out to greet us.
"Who are you?" and "Why are you here?", they asked excitedly.
I met so many of them that I couldn't remember their names.

Santa was so tired from his long trip that he went right to bed.
But the first thing he did the next morning was ask Captain Horatio Oldsalt to take
me around to meet everyone, learn their name, and find out what each elf did
to make the toys he would need for the next Christmas.
He also asked the old sea captain to tell me stories
about things that had happened in this village
so I could put them in my paper.

Captain Oldsalt is the elf in charge of making all of Santa's water toys,
so we went to his workshop first.
The elves were making every kind of water toy you could imagine.
There were big boats and little boats, sailboats and submarines,
and bathtub toys, too.

It didn't take long to learn that the captain likes to give special names
to things as well as people.
He calls his white whalers' coat his "Mobycoat" and his peg leg "Old Ahab".

Oldsalt took me from workshop to workshop to watch
the elves make racing cars and railroad trains,
building blocks and fishing poles,
and all kinds of balls.
There were so many different toys
that I didn't have time to play with them all,
but I tried.

All of the sewing is done in the Betsy Moss shop.
Her team of elves make doll clothes and dress-up clothes, costumes and flags,
and stuffed animals, too.

This is one of Captain Oldsalt's favorite workshops
since he can give a special name to each one of the stuffed animals.
The boys and girls that get them for Christmas can name them, too,
but they can only guess what their animals North Pole name was.

Oldsalt's special names for things and people
make the North Pole an even more fun place than I had guessed.
The Ikes Man is what he calls the elf that runs the shop
where all of the bikes, trikes, and unisikes are made.

Mushroom Heads is the name Oldsalt gave to the elves in Suzie Scheff's shop
because that's what their cooking hats look like.
They make all of the gum drops and lemon drops, candy canes and bubble gum,
and chocolate Santa Clauses, too.

It smelled so good in there that I wanted a bite of everything.
Sweet Suzie Scheff — she let me have all I wanted.

Oldsalt couldn't go with me when I went to the workshop where the jet planes and rocket ships, the gliders and kites, and the parachutes are made, so he told me to ask Will or Ollie Bright if I had any questions.
For Christmas, Santa needs so many flying toys that it takes both of the Bright brothers to make certain they are made just right.

Even though the elves test everything they make,
Santa Claus sometimes still delivers toys that don't work, but not often.

Oldsalt's favorite time to tell me stories about things that had happened in the villiage
was when he took me out to see the reindeer playing their games.
He told me lots of stories about things that happened all through the year.
After all, things don't happen at the North Pole just at Christmastime.

Sadly, even the best things can't last forever.
It seemed as if I had just gotten to his village when Santa said it was time for me to go home. He asked Captain Oldsalt to take me there in the little sleigh he uses when he doesn't have a big load of toys to carry.

As we started to leave,
I waved to all of the elves and reindeer who gathered to tell me good-bye.
I had a tear in my eye because I hated to leave them,
and because I knew I would probably never get to go to the North Pole again.

When I got home, I could hardly wait to see my family
and to start writing the newspapers for my friends.
I wanted to tell them about the elves I'd met and all of the things I'd seen.
But most of all, I wanted to write all of the exciting stories
that Captain Oldsalt had told me.

Of course I knew the big kids would never believe
I'd been lucky enough to go to the North Pole;
but I didn't care, my friends would.

My teacher once told me that chronicles was a big word that meant
"stories about things that had really happened",
so I changed the name of my paper to The North Pole Chronicles.